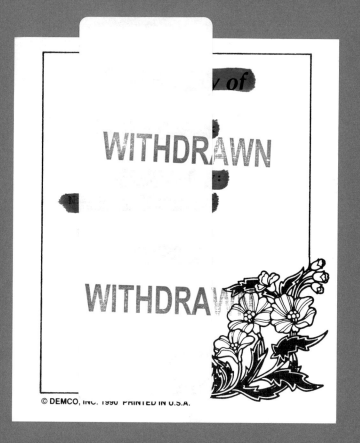

SONG

IT'S TIME TO

by Katherine Riley Nakamura

illustrated by Linnea Riley

THE BLUE SKY PRESS

An Imprint of Scholastic Inc. · New York

F NIGHT

GO TO BED

THE BLUE SKY PRESS

Text copyright © 2002 by Katherine Riley Nakamura

Illustrations copyright © 2002 by Linnea Riley

For information regarding permission, please write to:

Permissions Department, Scholastic Inc.,

555 Broadway, New York, New York 10012.

SCHOLASTIC, THE BLUE SKY PRESS, and associated logos

are trademarks and/or registered trademarks of Scholastic Inc.

Library of Congress catalog card number: 2001035991

ISBN 0-439-26678-5

10 9 8 7 6 5 4 3 2 1   02 03 04 05 06

Printed in Singapore   46

First printing, March 2002

Designed by Linnea Riley

and Kathleen Westray

For Bruce — K. R. N.

For Katie — L. R.

It's time for bed. Stars fill the skies.

Now it's time to close your eyes.

And now all children, just like you,

get ready for their bedtime, too.

Duckling bathes before lights out.

He splashes, washes, swims about.

Mice brush their teeth

without a care.

They make a mess

most everywhere.

Dogs will choose a bedtime song,

and everyone will sing along.

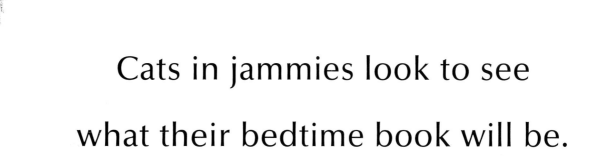

Cats in jammies look to see

what their bedtime book will be.

A skunk rubs Baby's back just so

while Daddy turns the lights down low.

Baby Bear

will softly sigh

as Daddy sings

a lullaby.

Mommy Squirrel sweetly hums

a loving song as slumber comes.

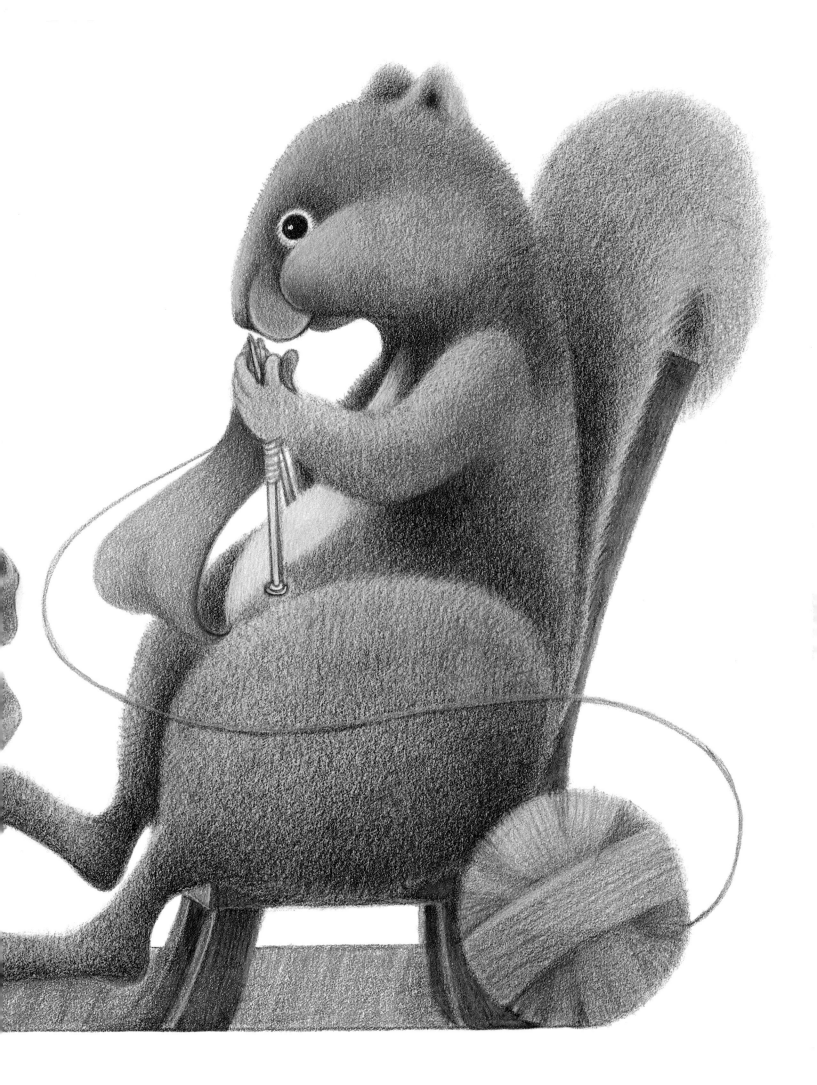

The moon is big and round and low.

Cloud boats sail, with stars in tow.

It's time for bed. Turn out your light

as crickets sing a song of night.

Moonbeams softly
light your bed.
Soon dreams fill
your sleepy head.

Close your eyes. To sleep you go.

Here's one more kiss. . . .

I love you so.